DARK MAN

THE FACE IN THE DARK MIRROR

BY PETER LANCETT

ILLUSTRATED BY JAN PEDROIETTA

Librarian Reviewer
Laurie K. Holland
Media Specialist (National Board Certified), Edina, MN
MA in Elementary Education, Minnesota State University, Mankato

Reading Consultant
Elizabeth Stedem
Educator/Consultant, Colorado Springs, CO
MA in Elementary Education, University of Denver, CO

STONE ARCH BOOKS
Minneapolis   San Diego

First published in the United States in 2008
by Stone Arch Books
151 Good Counsel Drive, P.O. Box 669
Mankato, Minnesota 56002
www.stonearchbooks.com

Library of Congress Cataloging-in-Publication Data
Lancett, Peter.
    The Face in the Dark Mirror / by Peter Lancett; illustrated by Jan
Pedroietta.
    p. cm. — (Zone Books. Dark Man)
    Summary: The Dark Man goes in search of the Dark Mirror, which
will reveal his true name.
    ISBN-13: 978-1-59889-868-2 (library binding)
    ISBN-10: 1-59889-868-X (library binding)
    ISBN-13: 978-1-59889-928-3 (paperback)
    ISBN-10: 1-59889-928-7 (paperback)
    [1. Good and evil—Fiction.] I. Pedroietta, Jan, ill. II. Title.
PZ7.L2313Fac 2008
[Fic]—dc22   2007003966

Art Director: Heather Kindseth
Graphic Designer: Kay Fraser

Photo Credits
Image Ideas, cover; Photo Disc, 13, 14, 15; Rubberball Visuality, 4, 16,
18, 19, 21, 23, 24

1 2 3 4 5 6 12 11 10 09 08 07

TABLE OF CONTENTS

In the dark and distant future, the Shadow Masters control the night. These evil powers threaten to cover the earth in complete darkness. One man has the power to stop them. He is the Dark Man — the world's only light of hope.

《 CHAPTER ONE 》

THE OLD MAN

The Dark Man was given a name.

That was a long time ago.

Now he is just the Dark Man.

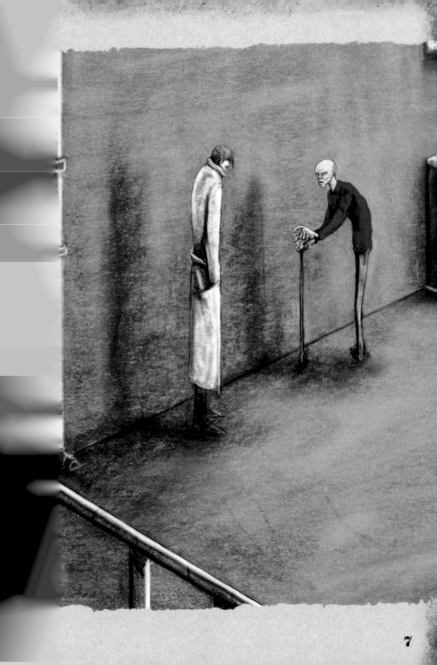

An Old Man told him to find the **Dark Mirror.**

"The Dark Mirror can tell names. **True names**."

That was what the Old Man said.

"How will I <u>know</u> the Dark Mirror?" the Dark Man asked.

"It will be in an evil place. A place of fear," said the Old Man.

CHAPTER TWO

A PLACE OF FEAR

So now the Dark Man is here, in a place of fear.

He is under the ground, below an old glass tower.

The glass tower is in the **city**.

The **glass tower** is in ruins.

Down here, the Dark Man must step with care.

There are no lamps down here.

The Old Man had
said more.

"Near the Dark Mirror, the walls can **bite**." the Old Man had said.

The Dark Man uses the back of his hand to **feel the walls**.

CHAPTER THREE

THE BITE

It is too **dark** to see down here.

All at once, the wall feels **warm**.

All at once, the wall feels **damp**.

The Dark Man pulls his
hands away.

There is a sound, like **sucking**.

The Dark Man's hands
are **slimy**.

It makes him **feel sick**.

Even so, he must feel the wall again.

He must find the Dark Mirror.

The Dark Man puts his hand **on** the wall.

He takes a step.

He feels **teeth** bite his hand.

《 CHAPTER FOUR 》

DESTINY

The Dark Man feels **sick** again.

But at least the Dark Mirror must be near.

The wall feels **smooth**, like glass.

It must be the Dark Mirror!

He cannot see **glass**.

He can see only **black**.

Then he sees a face.

A **face** in the Dark Mirror!

He knows that this is **magic**, but he is not afraid.

The face he sees is **his own**.

Then out of the **dark** he hears a soft word.

"David," it says.

The face in the Dark Mirror says the **word** again.

"**David**."

It is the name that the Dark
Man once had.

The Dark Man now has **his** **_old_**
name.

Yet as he turns to leave, he
cannot say why he now **feels sad**.

The end . . . for now.

MORE LIGHT ON MEMORY

Forgetting your name like the Dark Man is impossible, right? Maybe not. Here are a few quick facts about memory:

People with **amnesia** (am-NEE-zhuh) experience all types of memory loss. Amnesia is often caused by illness or injury.

A little memory loss is common with age. In fact, research has shown that young children actually have better memories than their parents.

How can you keep your memory sharp? Exercise your brain! The brain is a muscle, too. Keeping it active with puzzles, books, and other challenges will make it stronger.

Do you play a musical instrument? If so, you might do better on that math test. It's true. Scientists believe learning an instrument actually improves memory.

Eat more blueberries. These tiny fruits have been called "brain berries" because of their memory-boosting benefits.

Sea lions have the best memories of all animals. One smart sea lion, called Rio, remembered how to perform a trick 10 years after she had learned it.

ABOUT THE AUTHOR

Peter Lancett was born in the city of Stoke-on-Trent, England. At age 20, he moved to London. While there, he worked for a film studio and became a partner in a company producing music videos. He later moved to Auckland, New Zealand, where he wrote his first novel, *The Iron Maiden*. Today, Lancett is back in England and continues to write his ghoulish stories.

ABOUT THE ILLUSTRATOR

Jan Pedroietta lives and works in Germany. As a boy, Pedroietta always enjoyed drawing and creating things from his observations. He'd also spend hours reading his brother's western comic books about cowboys and American Indians. Today, comic artists still inspire Pedroietta as he continues improving his own skills.

GLOSSARY

damp (DAMP)—a little wet or moist

Dark Mirror (DARK MEER-ur)—a powerful mirror that can tell a person the truth about themselves

glass tower (GLASS TOU-ur)—a tall, shiny structure, which stands in the Dark Man's city. The Dark Mirror is hidden beneath the glass tower.

magic (MAJ-ik)—charms or spells that some people believe can make impossible things come true

power (POU-ur)—great strength, energy, or the ability to do something

ruins (ROO-inz)—the remains of something that has been nearly destroyed

DISCUSSION QUESTIONS

1. Do you think the Dark Man could have found the Dark Mirror without the Old Man? Name two ways that the Old Man helped him.

2. What are some of the challenges the Dark Man faced in the story? How did he overcome them? Why do you think the Dark Man didn't give up?

3. At the end of the story, the Dark Man finds out his old name. So why do you think he feels sad? What do you believe would make the Dark Man happy? Explain your answers.

INTERNET SITES

Do you want to know more about subjects related to this book? Or are you interested in learning about other topics? Then check out FactHound, a fun, easy way to find Internet sites.

Our investigative staff has already sniffed out great sites for you!

Here's how to use FactHound:

1. Visit *www.facthound.com*

2. Select your grade level.

3. To learn more about subjects related to this book, type in the book's ISBN number: **159889868X**.

4. Click the **Fetch It** button.

FactHound will fetch the best Internet sites for you!

WRITING PROMPTS

1. People's names often have interesting stories or meanings. Ask a parent or another adult about the history of your name. Write down any information or facts that you find.

2. The Old Man is a mysterious part of the story. Describe more about this character. Who do you think he is? How old is he? Where did he come from? How does he know the Dark Man?

3. The author doesn't give any information about David's past or how he became the Dark Man. Write your own story about David's childhood and how he turned into the Dark Man.